A Visit to
JAMAICA

by Charis Mather

Minneapolis, Minnesota

Credits

All images are courtesy of Shutterstock.com, unless otherwise specified. With thanks to Getty Images, Thinkstock Photo, and iStockphoto.

Cover – Lost Mountain Studio, Lucky-photographer. 2 – Lucky-photographer. 4-5 – George Brissett, ixpert. 6-7 – petch one, LBSimms Photography. 8-9 – Photo Spirit, Ievgenii Bakhvalov. 10-11 – Photo Spirit, Nenad Basic. 12-13 – Lost Mountain Studio, Photo Spirit. 14-15 – AS Food studio, Paul_Brighton. 16-17 – Jayne Lipkovich, Travelling Thilo. 18-19 – Vladimir Wrangel, Charles J. Sharp, CC BY-SA 4.0 <https://creativecommons.org/licenses/by-sa/4.0>, via Wikimedia Commons. 20-21 – photoyh, Salty View. 22-23 – Jam Travels, gmeland.

Library of Congress Cataloging-in-Publication Data is available at www.loc.gov or upon request from the publisher.

ISBN: 979-8-88509-374-3 (hardcover)
ISBN: 979-8-88509-496-2 (paperback)
ISBN: 979-8-88509-611-9 (ebook)

© 2023 Booklife Publishing
This edition is published by arrangement with Booklife Publishing.

North American adaptations © 2023 Bearport Publishing Company. All rights reserved. No part of this publication may be reproduced in whole or in part, stored in any retrieval system, or transmitted in any form or by any means, electronic, mechanical, photocopying, recording, or otherwise, without written permission from the publisher.

For more information, write to Bearport Publishing, 5357 Penn Avenue South, Minneapolis, MN 55419.

CONTENTS

Country to Country................. 4
Today's Trip Is to Jamaica! 6
Kingston and Port Royal............ 8
Blue Mountains................... 10
Reggae 12
Food............................ 14
Beaches 16
Animals 18
Sports........................... 20
Before You Go 22
Glossary......................... 24
Index............................ 24

COUNTRY TO COUNTRY

Which country do you live in?

A country is an area of land marked by **borders**. The people in each country have their own rules and ways of living. They may speak different languages.

Each country around the world has its own interesting things to see and do. Let's take a trip to visit a country and learn more!

Have you ever visited another country?

TODAY'S TRIP IS TO JAMAICA!

Jamaica is an island in the Caribbean Sea. This country is part of the **continent** of North America.

FACT FILE

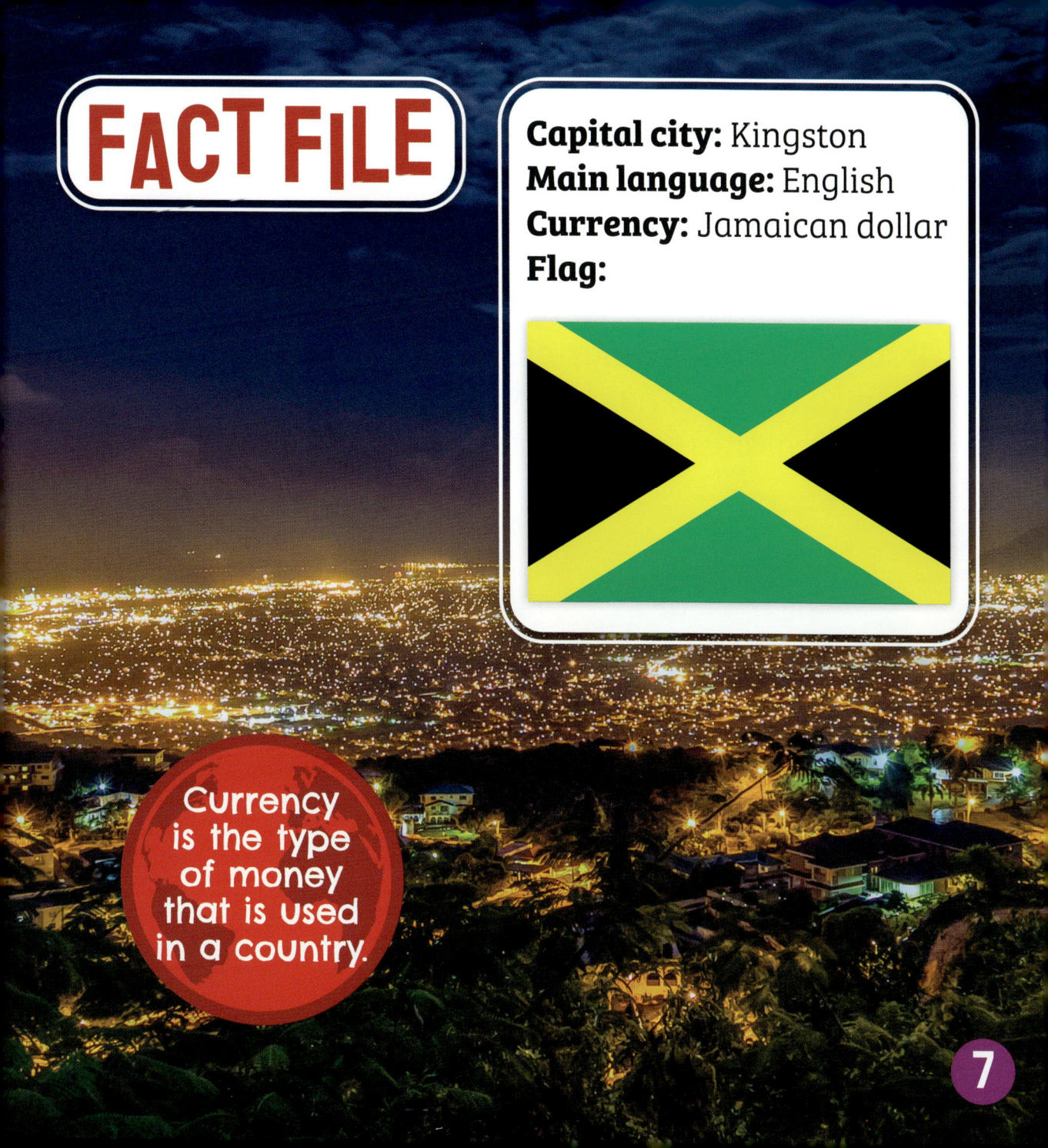

Capital city: Kingston
Main language: English
Currency: Jamaican dollar
Flag:

Currency is the type of money that is used in a country.

7

KINGSTON AND PORT ROYAL

We'll start our trip in Kingston, the capital of Jamaica. This city has lots of museums and historical sites for people to visit.

Port Royal sunk into the sea because of an **earthquake**.

Near Kingston, we can stop by a little town where pirates used to stay! Port Royal was once a busy place, but most of the town sunk under water hundreds of years ago. Now, people visit what is left to learn about Port Royal's history.

BLUE MOUNTAINS

Next, we'll head to the Blue Mountains, the highest point in Jamaica. The tallest **peak** is more than 7,400 feet (2,250 m) high. Many streams and waterfalls flow down the mountainsides.

There are many different kinds of plants on the Blue Mountains. This area is especially known for the coffee plants that people grow there.

The coffee people drink is made from seeds in the fruit of coffee plants.

11

REGGAE

Let's listen to some music! A popular style of music called reggae started in Jamaica. Reggae has a strong **rhythm** led by drums and bass guitar.

This music is so important to Jamaica that the country officially celebrates February as Reggae Month.

Kingston has a museum about Bob Marley, a famous reggae musician.

FOOD

Jerk chicken

Feeling hungry? Let's try some jerk chicken. This popular Jamaican dish is covered in spices and cooked slowly over a fire.

We could also try ackee and saltfish. This dish looks like it is made of egg, but it is actually made from a yellow fruit cooked with fish. People in Jamaica eat ackee and saltfish for any meal of the day.

Ackee and saltfish

BEACHES

Want to go to the beach? On an island like Jamaica, there are plenty of them! The country's **coastline** is hundreds of miles long. It has many beaches where people relax or go swimming.

Negril Beach

Large beaches, such as Negril Beach, have several restaurants and hotels for people to visit. Other beaches, such as Frenchman's Cove, are much smaller.

Frenchman's Cove

ANIMALS

While we're at the beach, we might see a manatee! These large animals live in waters around Jamaica. They swim up to the surface about every five minutes to breathe air.

Jamaica is also home to hundreds of kinds of birds. Some can be found only in Jamaica. The country's **national** bird is the red-billed streamertail, which is known for its long tail feathers.

SPORTS

Shelly-Ann Fraser

Time for sports! The most popular sports in Jamaica are track and field, soccer, and **cricket**.

Usain Bolt

Jamaican athletes have become famous all over the world. Shelly-Ann Fraser and Usain Bolt are two of the fastest runners ever. Usain has broken several **sprinting** world records.

BEFORE YOU GO

We can't forget to visit the Martha Brae River. Taking a long bamboo **raft** down the river is a good way to see the Jamaican rain forest.

We could also go to Dunn's River Falls. These beautiful waterfalls have lots of round rocks that look like stairs. The water flows down them and into the Caribbean Sea.

What have you learned about Jamaica on this trip?

23

GLOSSARY

borders lines that show where one place ends and another begins

coastline where the edge of land meets water

continent one of the world's seven large areas of land

cricket a sport played with a ball and bat on a large field

earthquake a sudden shaking of the land on Earth

national something relating to an entire country

peak the top of a mountain

raft a flat boat, often made of wood, used to travel across water

rhythm a pattern of sounds that repeats

sprinting running very fast for a short distance

INDEX

beaches 16–18
birds 19
coffee 11
food 14–15
manatees 18
mountains 10–11
reggae 12–13
sports 20–21
waterfalls 10, 23